# The Story of Peas & Carrots

Written by

Leanne A. Gelish

ISBN: **978-0997168129**

*Dedicated to all the kids who refused to eat their peas and carrots.*

There once was a farmer named Pete,
Who wanted to grow anything but beets.
He tried all different types of methods,
But nothing grew like he expected.

He sowed the seeds,
He watered the mulch,
And one day, there was a bulge.

A little plant began to grow,
And, Pete was all aglow!

For days, and days he would watch in awe,
Until one day, this new plant was two inches tall.

There on the stem he saw this little pod-like ball.
He ate it, and its flavor wasn't what he expected at all!

Pete grew lots and lots of this new vegetable.
But, all of the townspeople were skeptical.
He begged and pleaded for them to "try just one, please!"
And all his pleas, started to sound like "peas".

"That's it!" Pete chimed.
He would name this new vegetable "peas"
And, then people would eat it all the time.

Soon, 'Pete's Pea Farm' became the talk of the town,
This meant he was busy until the sun went down.

Pete was so happy.
With all of his savvy,
Surely nothing could hurt his farm.

Until one day a new vegetable came to town,
'Carrie's Carrot Farm' was ready for a hoedown!
All so cheery with their favorite vegetable: peas.
No one would try something new, "YUCK! Geez!".

That all changed when a little boy named Steve,
Decided to test Carrie's Carrots Farm's expertise.
He grabbed this orange vegetable from the root,
And, looked at it quite astute.

He took a big bite! "Crunch! "
"Yum! This is delicious." he declared.
Soon, everyone was eating carrots everywhere!

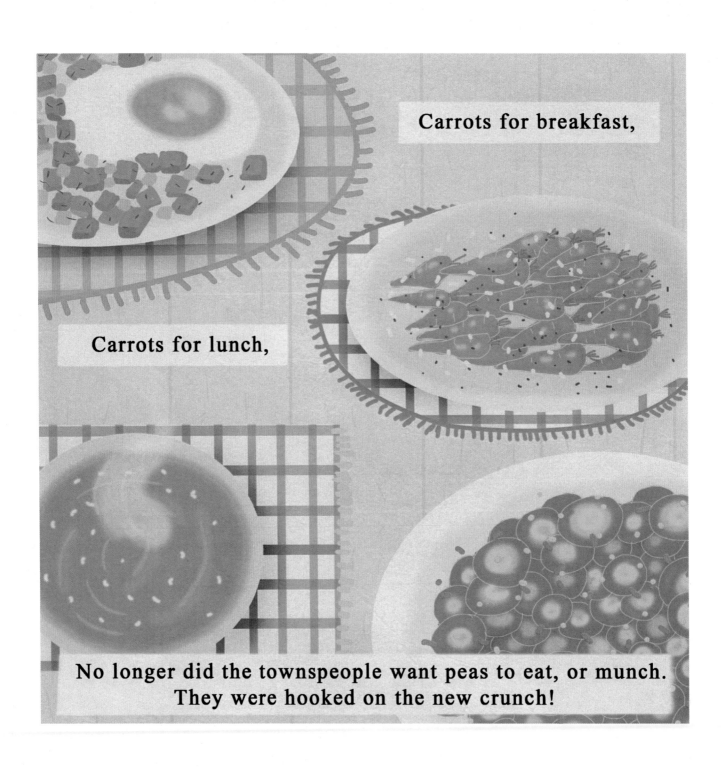

Carrots for breakfast,

Carrots for lunch,

No longer did the townspeople want peas to eat, or munch.
They were hooked on the new crunch!

Pete watched as his farm slowly withered,
For his peas were no longer considered.

On her morning walk to town,
Carrie saw a man who looked quite down.

"Whats wrong?" she questioned.
For this man looked like he was in quite the depression.

"The carrots have taken all of my business." Pete replied, "But wait, Pete! I love your peas! This was certainly not my vision." Carrie stated as tears welled in her eyes.

Carrie didn't want to ruin another farm,
Instead, she had an idea that could turn out to be a
good luck charm.

"Pete, do you have any more peas?" Carrie asked,
Pete replied: "I only have a few,
but they're dying pretty fast."

"Grab all the peas you have and follow me!"
Carrie exclaimed.

Finally, it was time for the peas to reclaim their fame.

Both farmers filled their baskets with lots of peas,
When they arrived at the carrot farm
they were up to their knees in peas!

Carrie grouped both the peas and carrots together,
Telling all her morning customers the two tasted
better together.

The townspeople loved the taste and texture,
The peas and carrots became quite the hunger-quencher!

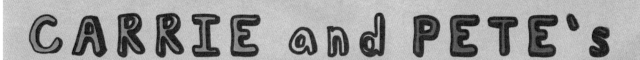

# CARRIE and PETE's

peas and

Carrie and Pete went into business.
Selling their peas and carrots,
Became a beautiful thing to witness.

The story of peas and carrots is quite ambitious
However, no one can deny that together,
they're quite delicious

So the next time you're told to eat your vegetables,
Remember, it was Pete and Carrie who made them so credible!

The End.

## ABOUT THE AUTHOR

Leanne Gelish is the author of several children's books, including *"Audrey & the Extraordinary Camera"*. When she is not imagining stories, Leanne can be found dappling in photography, exploring her home, Long Island, with her husband Mark & their dog, Emmett, or simply enjoying the beach.

You can find other work by Leanne on Amazon.

Made in the USA
Las Vegas, NV
01 September 2022

54539789R00019